Blackmail!

"You've never even been to Krad!" Darek shouted to Zarnak. "How can you lead a rescue?"

Zarnak came over and put an arm around Darek's shoulders. He smiled down wickedly. "Very easily, my young friend," he said. "You and your dragon will guide me."

"I'll not guide you anywhere," Darek spat.

"Oh, but I think you will," Zarnak whispered. "You see, it's up to *me* how your father and brother spend their year in prison. And may I remind you, some of our prison cells are . . . shall we say . . . more *comfortable* than others?"

Darek's blood ran cold. He remembered all too clearly the dungeons of Elder Hall.

"You wouldn't," he said in a hoarse whisper.

Zarnak's mouth widened into an evil grin. "Oh, but I *would*," he said with a low, menacing laugh.

Available from MINSTREL Books

Visit Zantor on the Internet:
http://members.aol.com/zantor1/index.htm

Dragons
and Kings

Jackie French Koller

Illustrated by Judith Mitchell

A
MINSTREL®
BOOK

Published by POCKET BOOKS
New York   London   Toronto   Sydney   Tokyo   Singapore

13551431

A MINSTREL PAPERBACK *Original*

A Minstrel Book published by
POCKET BOOKS, a division of Simon & Schuster Inc.
1230 Avenue of the Americas, New York, NY 10020

ISBN: 0-671-01400-5

First Minstrel Books printing January 1998

10 9 8 7 6 5 4 3 2 1

A MINSTREL BOOK and colophon are registered trademarks of
Simon & Schuster Inc.

Cover art by Judith Mitchell

Printed in the U.S.A.

Dragons and Kings

Prologue

When Darek decided to rescue a baby Blue dragon from certain death, he had no idea that he was about to change his world forever. Darek's friendship with Zantor the dragon has brought one problem after another—problems with family, problems with friends, problems with Darek's whole village. But now it has led to the biggest problem of all.

When Zantor and Darek's best friend, Pola, disappeared into the dreaded Black Mountains of Krad, Darek and his friend Rowena went after them. The fathers of the three children and Darek's brother, Clep, soon followed. For a time all were enslaved in Krad. But with the help of Zantor, they finally escaped, only to be arrested upon their return to Zoriac. It is against the law for Zorians to venture into the Black Mountains. The law was made to keep Zorians from danger, and to be sure they did not disturb the mythical Kradens whom some believed lived there.

Darek and the others have discovered that the cruel Kradens are indeed real and that they keep Zorians as slaves. Darek and the others hope to go back and rescue the slaves, but first they must stand trial.

Darek, Pola, and Rowena are soon pardoned. They are only ten, too young to be sentenced. But their fathers and Clep face imprisonment, or even death. Especially if Zarnak has his way. Zarnak has been acting as Chief Elder while Rowena's father, the true Chief, has been away. It is a job Zarnak would like to keep. Now the trials are under way and the whole village waits. How will the Elders decide?

1

Something bumped Darek's back and he shot up in bed, wide awake, heart pounding. A forked tongue flicked out and kissed him on the cheek. Darek smiled and gave a sigh of relief.

"Oh, it's you, Zantor," he said. "Sorry I'm so jumpy. I didn't sleep much last night, worrying about the trial."

"*Grrrawwk*," said Zantor.

Darek rubbed the gentle dragon's nose. Zantor was fully grown now, too big to fit in the house anymore. Instead, he camped under Darek's win-

3

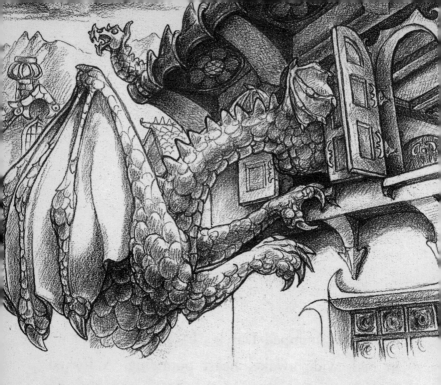

dow at night and awakened Darek each morning by pushing his great head in through the window. His voice had changed too. His baby distress cry of "Rrrronk" had become a full-throated *"Grrrawwk,"* and his joyful *thrummm*s were so loud now they shook the house.

Zantor nudged him again, as if to say, "Let's go."

"I'm not in the mood for a ride this morning,

Zantor," Darek said quietly. "Today the verdicts will be announced."

"*Grrrawwk*," said Zantor, hanging his head. He looked so sad that Darek relented.

"All right," he said. "Just a short one."

Zantor's eyes lit up. "*Thrummm,*" he sang.

"Shussh." Darek couldn't help giggling as his bed started to vibrate across the floor. "You'll bounce Mother right out of bed." He slipped into his breeches, then threw his arms around Zantor's neck.

"Let's go," he cried.

Zantor ducked out of the window, then unfurled his silver wings. With one spring of his great legs they were airborne. Up, up they rose, until Darek's house looked like a little toy. Zoriak's violet sun was warm on Darek's back. Clean, fresh air filled his lungs and whipped at his hair. It was so good to be home, free from the gray, smoky skies of Krad. They circled the barnyard and struck off across the valley. In the morning stillness of a pond below, Darek caught sight of

Zantor's reflection. He was magnificent! Darek couldn't help smiling as he recalled the day he had given the tiny, trembling dragonling his name. "I will give you a strong name," he remembered saying, "a powerful name. I will call you Zantor, King of the Dragons." It had seemed back then that the name would never fit. Now it fit perfectly. Zantor was everything a king should be. He was powerful and strong, but he was good, too. Not like Zarnak, who was trying to steal the throne from Rowena's father. Or Zahr, the terrible king of Krad.

Darek shivered, recalling his slave days in Krad. His heart grew heavy at the thought of the other slaves he had left behind. They still labored day and night for the cruel Zahr.

"If only Azzon were king again," Darek said half aloud. "Azzon would set them free." Azzon had once been king of all Krad. He had been cruel then, too—so cruel that he'd raised his sons Zahr and Rebbe like beasts. When they grew older they had turned on each other, then on him, and Azzon had fled into the Black Mountains. He would have died there in the poisonous mists, but the gentle Zynots who lived in the mountains had saved him. Their kindness had changed Azzon into a good and gentle man. Now Zahr ruled Krad in the north and Rebbe in the south, not knowing or caring that their father still lived in hiding beneath the Black Mountains.

Someday, Darek promised himself, he would go back and help his slave friends in Krad. But now he had more pressing worries. His father and brother were on trial, along with Pola's father and Rowena's. If found guilty they could be put to death, and the verdict would be decided this very day.

2

Darek felt very small seated at the great council table. Overhead the fierce faces of long-dead dragons glared at him. Their skins covered the walls. Their tails trailed across the ceiling. On either side of Darek sat Pola and Rowena, looking just as small and scared as he. Behind them, in a second row of chairs, sat their mothers.

"All rise," boomed a loud voice.

Darek jumped to his feet as Zarnak, the acting Chief Elder, strode into the room. Behind him came the Council of Elders. Last came Horek, the dep-

uty captain of the guards, leading Darek's father and brother, Pola's father, and Xylon, the Chief Elder.

Zarnak took his place upon the Dragon Throne while the Elders filed into the chairs on either side of the council table. Darek tried to read their stony faces. Yesterday, Zarnak had called for a guilty verdict. But which Elders supported Zarnak, and which Xylon? There was no way to know.

The prisoners were seated directly across the table from Darek, Pola, and Rowena. Then the Deputy Captain went and stood at attention beside the throne. Darek hated to see the man standing in his father's place. He glanced at Rowena and knew she was feeling the same way. She glared at Zarnak, who sat upon her father's throne.

"Please, Lord Eternal," Darek whispered to himself. "Let the verdict go in our favor."

Two heralds stepped through the great doors at the end of the room and lifted their horns.

"Ta-da-da-da-da-DA!" the horns sounded.

10

Then Zarnak stood and unfurled a scroll. Darek held his breath.

"The exalted Council of Elders," Zarnak droned, "has met and considered this case in accordance with the laws of Zoriac." An evil gleam came into his eyes, and Darek's heart sank. "A verdict has been returned," he went on. "Guilty as charged!"

Darek felt like a fist had slammed into his stomach. Behind him he heard a small cry escape his mother's lips. Rowena was less discreet.

"No!" she cried out, but a sharp look from her father silenced her.

None of the fathers flinched at the verdict, but Darek's brother, Clep, turned pale. It was a hard blow for a boy of thirteen. Darek saw tears in his brother's eyes. Tears started behind Darek's eyes, too, and he looked down so his father and Clep would not see.

"Furthermore and notwithstanding," Zarnak went on, "the Council has taken the following facts into account. Fact one: The first child, Pola,

11

was carried into the Black Mountains by a runaway wagon against his will. Fact two: The second and third children, Darek and Rowena, entered the Black Mountains out of concern for the first child. Fact three: The four defendants entered the Black Mountains out of concern for all three children."

A sour look had settled over Zarnak's features, and Darek began to feel a glimmer of hope.

"In consideration of these facts," Zarnak announced, "the sentence is hereby reduced to imprisonment in the dungeons of Elder Hall for one anum."

Darek closed his eyes and sank back in his chair. A year in prison. It was still uncalled for, in his opinion, but it could have been so much worse. He felt his mother's hand on his shoulder and he reached up and squeezed it.

3

Zarnak announced the verdict in the village square that afternoon. Darek had hoped the villagers would protest the sentence, but they did not. He listened to the low buzz of conversation around him. It was a fair sentence, the people murmured. A law was a law, after all, and everyone, even a Chief Elder, had to pay some price for breaking one.

Darek sighed and turned to Pola and Rowena. "So what do we do now?" he asked.

"About what?" asked Pola.

"About Krad and the slaves," said Darek.

Pola and Rowena shook their heads. "We'll have to wait," said Rowena, "until our fathers are free again."

"Yes," Pola agreed. "It will probably take that long to plan a rescue anyway."

Darek nodded thoughtfully. "Come to think of it," he said, "that might work out perfectly. A year from now will be Spirit season again."

Rowena's and Pola's eyes brightened. Spirit season occurred each spring in Krad, when the weather grew warm and the ground was still cold. For a few nights the mountain mists settled low in the valleys. The Kradens were forced to stay indoors, but the Zynots, who breathed the mist, were free to come down out of the mountains. They ran through the dark streets shrieking and howling, terrifying the Kradens, who believed they were evil spirits.

"Yes!" Rowena cried. "That would be the perfect time! The Zynots could help us rescue the slaves!"

"We might just be able to pull the whole thing off without bloodshed," said Pola.

"THERE IS ANOTHER MATTER!" Zarnak suddenly boomed from the platform in the middle of the square. "ONE WHICH REQUIRES OUR IMMEDIATE ATTENTION."

The faces of the crowd turned upward again.

"As we now know," said Zarnak gravely, "the Kradens are real. They are not creatures of myth, but beings like us. They are large and dangerous, to be sure, but not invincible."

The crowd murmured and nodded.

"There is something more you must know," said Zarnak. "Something terrible." He paused, then went on in a loud, dramatic voice. "There are Zorians in Krad, Zorian slaves!"

A gasp went up from the crowd and voices began to buzz in astonishment.

Darek frowned. "Why is he telling them that now?" he whispered to Pola and Rowena. "Why get them all riled up while our fathers are in prison?"

15

"I don't know," Rowena returned worriedly, "but I'm getting a bad feeling."

"These people are our kin," Zarnak was shouting. "Blood of our blood, descended from common ancestors."

The buzzing of the crowd grew louder.

"They are being held in dire conditions," Zarnak went on. "They are whipped, beaten, made to labor day and night. Their children are torn from their arms and put to work as soon as they can walk!"

Fists began to be raised in the air.

"Free the Zorians!" one man shouted.

"Death to the Kradens!" another cried.

Rowena suddenly whirled. "Zatz," she said to Pola and Darek. "Don't you see what he's up to? *He* wants to rescue the Zorians. He wants to be a hero. . . ."

Pola and Darek stared at her, then nodded slowly. "So the people will make him Chief Elder," said Pola. "So he can gain the throne for himself before your father is free again!"

Zarnak went on shouting about the plight of the slaves. He was whipping the crowd into a frenzy.

"Wait!" Darek cried. "No! You can't do this!" But his voice was lost in the uproar. "Pola, Rowena," he cried. "Help me up onto the platform!"

Pola and Rowena linked hands and gave Darek a boost. He hoisted himself up onto the platform, then stood and waved his arms.

"Hear me!" he cried. "Please hear me!"

Zarnak cocked an eye in his direction. "Seize him!" he shouted to one of his guards.

"NO!" came a piercing cry from the crowd.

There was a sudden hush as Rowena's mother, the Grand Dame, strode forward. Behind her were Darek's mother and Pola's.

"What are you afraid of, Zarnak?" she asked, looking up. "Why won't you let the boy speak? He has been to Krad, after all. Have you?"

"She's right," someone shouted.

"Yes," cried another. "Hear the boy out!"

"As you wish, milady" said Zarnak through

clenched teeth. He tilted his head to the Grand Dame, then turned and glared at Darek. "Speak!"

Darek swallowed hard, then looked down at the crowd. "It's true that the slaves need help," he said. "But a rescue must be carefully planned. It will take time. . . ."

"How much time?" snarled Zarnak. "An anum perhaps?"

"Per-perhaps," said Darek.

"Nonsense!" Zarnak boomed. "The boy is speaking for his father, don't you see? And the Grand Dame for her husband. Of course Xylon and Yanek want us to wait. Of course *they* want to lead the rescue, to be the heroes! But what of the slaves who are dying even now? What of the Zorian children crying in Krad this very day? Can *they* wait? *Should* they wait while our would-be heroes serve their time in prison?"

The crowd heated up again. "No!" people shouted. "Free them now! Save the children! Death to the Kradens! Death to Zahr!"

"But you've never even been to Krad!" Darek

shouted to Zarnak. "You know nothing about it! How can you lead a rescue?"

Zarnak came over and put an arm around Darek's shoulders. He smiled down wickedly. "Very easily, my young friend," he said. "You and your dragon will guide me."

"I'll not guide you anywhere," Darek spat.

"Oh, I think you will." Zarnak lowered his lips until they were right next to Darek's ear. "You see, the Elders have decreed how much time your father and brother will spend in prison. But it's up to me *how* they spend it. And may I remind you, some of our prison cells are . . . shall we say . . . more *comfortable* than others?

Darek's blood ran cold. He thought back to the day, not long ago, when he and Pola had sneaked into the dungeons of Elder Hall. He remembered all too clearly the dank, dark solitary confinement cells, barely big enough for a man to lie down in.

"You wouldn't," he said in a hoarse whisper.

Zarnak's mouth widened into an evil grin. "Oh, but I *would*," he said with a low, menacing laugh.

4

The village seemed flush with new life. Not since the days of the dragon quests had Darek seen so much activity. The women were busy making battle masks. The men were minting swords and stringing bows. The alehouses were full to bursting each night with men singing songs and telling tales of brave deeds of long ago.

"It's like they're happy," said Darek as he sat in the garden watching his mother stitch straps for the battle masks. "Don't they know how dangerous it's going to be? Don't they know they could be killed?"

Alayah sighed and dropped her hands in her lap. She looked into Darek's eyes and struggled to find the right words to say to him.

"There *is* a bloodlust about men," she said at last. "It harks back, I think, to the Long Ago, when men were little more than beasts and had to fight to live." She looked at a group of boys out in the lane, charging each other with wooden swords. "It sits in men's hearts like a smoldering ember," she went on, "ever waiting to be fanned into fury." Darek heard and knew the truth of his mother's words. He had felt that ember within his own young heart. Before Zantor came into his life, Darek had dreamed of joining a dragon quest. He had itched for the thrill of battle, longed to make the kill, and wear the prize, a dragon claw necklace, about his neck.

"Grrrawwk," said Zantor softly. Darek put a hand on the dragon's head. They shared a special bond and often knew each other's thoughts.

"Don't worry, Zantor," he said. "Those days are behind me." He looked at his mother again.

"Men will die on both sides," he said quietly. "And there is no need. Only Zarnak's greed for power."

Alayah smiled sadly. "I fear, my son," she said softly, "that greed is at the root of most wars."

Darek stood up and paced the length of the garden. A guard, posted by Zarnak, watched his every move. Darek turned and paced back again.

"We've got to stop them," he said in a low voice. He quit pacing and turned to his mother. "Can't you do anything?" he asked. "You and the Grand Dame? Can't you talk to the other women?"

Alayah shook her head. "We're under guard, too, don't forget. Besides, the people believe Zarnak. They say we think only of your father and Clep. They say we must think of the slaves in Krad."

Darek bent and put his hands on the arms of his mother's chair. "I *am* thinking of the slaves," he said. "They'll die too. It's going to be a bloodbath. Don't you understand?"

23

Alayah's eyes filled with tears. "All too well," she said, looking away. "And you will be in the thick of it."

Darek bit his lip, angry with himself. His mother had enough on her mind. He hadn't meant to burden her further. He took her hands and squeezed them. "Don't you worry about Zantor and me," he said gently. "We know how to take care of ourselves." Then he looked over at the dragon and added, "Don't we, boy?"

"Thrummm," sang Zantor. He swung his great head over and licked the tears from Alayah's cheek.

There was a sudden clattering out on the street and another guard rode up. He dismounted and approached Darek.

"Your presence is required at Elder Hall," he said.

5

Pola and Rowena were already seated when Darek arrived. Zarnak was on the throne and Horek at his side.

"Ah, young Darek," said Zarnak in a falsely sweet voice. "We've been waiting for you. Do sit down."

Darek slid into a chair across from Rowena. *What is this all about?* he asked her with his eyes.

I have no idea, her eyes replied.

A glance from Pola told Darek he was equally puzzled.

"I suppose you're all wondering why you're here," said Zarnak.

Darek, Pola, and Rowena said nothing.

"Come, come now," said Zarnak. "This hostility will get us nowhere." He smiled wickedly. "Can't we all be friends?"

The three glared at him in silence.

"All right then," Zarnak snapped. "Have it your way. But you *will* cooperate, like it or not! We are going to Krad and you are coming with us. And we are *not* coming home without the slaves. So wipe those scowls off your faces and let's get down to business."

Darek, Pola, and Rowena glared on.

"Horek," boomed Zarnak. "The wretches need convincing. Get the prisoners—"

"No!" Darek leaned forward. "No," he said. "Leave the prisoners alone. We'll cooperate."

Zarnak arched a brow, then looked at Rowena and Pola. They both nodded.

"All right, then. Your fathers have told us much

about Krad. We need to know if they are speaking the truth."

Rowena frowned. "My father wouldn't lie," she snapped. "Do you think he would mislead his own people? Even to get back at you?"

"That remains to be seen," said Zarnak. "Now, tell me all you know of Krad."

Pola and Rowena turned to Darek. He took a deep breath and began. "Krad is a great basin," he said, "ringed on all sides by mountains. A thick mist of dragonsbreath clings to the mountains. This mist is deadly to Kradens and addles the minds of Zorians. Harmless little creatures called Zynots live in the mountains. They are descended from Zorians whose minds were addled long ago."

"Yes, yes," said Zarnak impatiently. "We know all that. The mist is of no concern as long as we wear our battle masks. I want to know about the Kraden forces. How strong are they?"

Darek and his friends exchanged glances.

"We have no idea how many men they have,"

he said. "Enough, to be sure. And we know nothing of the Southern Kingdom—the one Rebbe rules. There are slaves there, too. But we have only seen the Northern Kingdom—Zahr's."

"We will worry about the Northern Kingdom first," Zarnak said. "Once we have conquered Zahr we will turn our attention to Rebbe."

Darek's eyes widened. "Conquer?" he said. "You plan to *conquer* Zahr?"

"Of course," said Zarnak. "How else would we free the slaves?"

"There may be another way," Rowena put in.

Zarnak narrowed his eyes. "And what might that be?"

"If we could just wait for Spirit season . . ." she began.

"No waiting!" Zarnak boomed. "We leave as soon as possible." He turned back to Darek. "They say you're a natural-born leader," he said. "Tell me. How would *you* conquer Zahr?"

Darek shook his head. "I don't see any way," he said. "The Kradens are bigger and stronger than we are. And they have a powerful weapon—the Red Fanged dragons. We have but three fighting dragons in all Zoriac. Our Great Blues. One on one a Blue might be able to defeat a Red. But the Kradens have a herd of hundreds . . . . We don't stand a chance. Unless . . ."

Zarnak leaned forward eagerly. "Unless what?"

Darek sat back and chewed his lip thoughtfully. "Unless we capture the Red Fangs," he said.

Zarnak sat back, too. A slow smile curled his lips. "Horek," he said, "prepare our departure."

6

In two days' time all was in readiness. A battle force of over a thousand men was outfitted and eager to move out. The day of departure dawned bright and clear. Darek was to lead the way, on Zantor. Zarnak and Horek followed on Pola and Rowena's dragons, Drizba and Typra.

Pola, Rowena, and the rest of the men were to follow on yukes. Darek glanced at his two friends, beside their yukes, and saw the anger smoldering in their eyes. At least Darek was being allowed to ride Zantor. That was something to be grateful for.

"All mount!" came Horek's shouted command at last. Darek kissed his mother good-bye and she clung to him tightly for a moment. When she drew away, there were tears in her eyes.

"Stay well," she said softly.

"I will," Darek promised her. Then he grabbed the mounting rope that hung from Zantor's saddle and climbed up onto the dragon's back. He lowered his battle mask and patted Zantor's neck. "Well, old friend," he said, "as Pola always says, an adventure's an adventure, all the way to the end. Looks like we're on our way again."

The dragons flew slowly, keeping just ahead of the yukes. By late afternoon they had gained the mountain peak and begun their descent. "I'd suggest making camp here," Darek called out at dusk. "The lower we go, the thinner the mist. Soon the Kraden guards will be able to see us."

Zarnak nodded and gave the signal to land.

"Pass the word to your men," Darek told

Horek. "Tell them to take their masks off only long enough to eat. The mist sneaks up on you."

A guard brought Pola and Rowena forward.

"You'll camp with us," Zarnak told them. "I want the three of you where I can keep my eye on you."

Rowena snorted. "Aren't we lucky," she said. She yanked her arm out of the guard's grip and sat down on a log. "When do we eat?" she asked. "I'm starving."

Zarnak chuckled, then handed her a pot and a plucked zok. "Just as soon as you cook," he said. "I do so enjoy food prepared with a woman's touch."

"Really?" said Rowena. She flung the zok back in Zarnak's face. "There, I touched it. Enjoy!"

Zarnak lunged and grabbed her arm. "Look, you little wench," he said. "You may be used to getting your own way. But those days are over. *I'm* Chief Elder now."

"No, you're not," snapped Rowena. "Not as long as my father lives."

Zarnak chuckled. "You'd best behave," he said in a low voice. "Or that may not be very long." Then he jerked her to her feet and handed her the zok again. "Make a stew," he said. "And don't get any funny ideas. We'll all be eating out of the same pot."

Then he turned and pointed To Darek and Pola. "Make a campfire!" he bellowed.

Under the watchful eye of a guard, Darek and Pola set about gathering sticks. Then Darek called Zantor to breathe on the pile. Soon Rowena's stew was bubbling. She ladled it into bowls and passed it around and they all began to eat.

"What was that?" Zarnak suddenly asked.

"What?" asked Darek.

"I thought I heard something." Zarnak looked around warily. "I get the feeling something is watching us."

"Something is," said Darek. "Lots of some-things. The Zynots. They're wondering who you are and what you want."

"Why don't they show themselves?" asked Zarnak.

"They don't trust you," said Darek.

"They're good judges of character," Rowena added.

Pola and Darek smiled into their bowls.

Zarnak snorted and went back to his meal. "Well, if they know what's good for them, they'll stay out of my way," he said.

"They will," boomed a sudden loud voice. "But I won't!"

Zarnak dropped his plate and stared up at the huge masked figure that had just emerged from the mist.

7

"Azzon!" cried Darek, Pola, and Rowena at once.
They all jumped up.

Zarnak jumped up, too.

"You know this creature?" he demanded of
Darek and his friends.

"Yes. He's the rightful King of Krad," said
Darek.

Zarnak's eyes widened. "Take him prisoner!"
he shouted to the guards. They closed in with
spears raised. Suddenly out of the shadows leaped
dozens of small, gray-scaled creatures. With loud

shrieks and howls they starting kicking the guards and throwing rocks at them. The guards began to thrust back at the creatures with their spears.

"STOP!" bellowed Azzon. He eyed the creatures angrily, but when he spoke there was a note of fondness in his voice. "Out of here, now!" he commanded, "before you get hurt."

Reluctantly, the creatures slipped back into the shadows. The guards closed in on Azzon again.

"No!" Rowena came forward and grabbed the nearest spear. "Azzon is a friend."

"*Was* a friend," said Azzon. He looked hard at Darek, Pola, and Rowena. Then he looked around him at the camp and the regiments that stretched back into the hills. "Friends don't break promises," he added quietly.

Darek's cheeks grew hot. Azzon had helped them many times. In return, they had promised never to bring harm to his sons.

"I'm sorry, Azzon," he said. "This is not our doing."

"Silence!" Zarnak interrupted. "What are you talking about? How do you know this Kraden?"

"If you'll allow Azzon to sit and eat with us," said Rowena, "I'll explain."

Zarnak pondered a moment, then nodded. The guards backed off enough for Azzon to sit down. Rowena then launched into the story of Azzon and his sons, and how Azzon came to be living beneath the mountain.

"Where did he get that battle mask?" Zarnak demanded.

"We gave it to him on our last trip," said Pola. "To thank him for his help. It allows him to spend time up here with the Zynots."

"That was foolish," said Zarnak. "What if he gave it to his sons? What if they—"

"As you have been told," Azzon interrupted, "I am estranged from my sons. They don't know I'm

39

alive. If they did, they would kill me first chance they got."

Zarnak stared at Azzon and pulled at his chin thoughtfully. "In that case," he said, "perhaps you can be of use to us. You could help—"

"No," Azzon snapped. "I am to blame for what my sons are. I hold no anger toward them. I love them, and I will not be a party to your plans."

Zarnak frowned. "Chain him, then!" he shouted to the guards.

Darek, Pola, and Rowena watched helplessly as Azzon's hands and feet were locked into irons. Azzon would not even meet their eyes.

Scuffling and mumbling sounds were heard in the bushes.

Zarnak turned toward the sounds. "As for all of you!" he shouted.

"*Sire,*" said Darek loudly.

Zarnak whirled. "*What?*"

Darek walked over to Zarnak and spoke qui-

etly. "You'd be wise not to send the Zynots away," he said. "They know these hills better than anyone."

Zarnak stared at him thoughtfully. "Yes," he said. "You have a point." He turned toward the mist again. "Zynots!" he shouted. "If you don't wish to see your friend Azzon harmed, then I expect your full cooperation. Come forth now."

There was only silence. Zarnak pulled a dagger

from his belt and walked over to Azzon. He put it to the big man's throat.

"NOW!" he bellowed.

Slowly the Zynots began to emerge. A very small one sidled up to Darek and grabbed his hand. Darek looked down and smiled.

"Hello, Mizzle," he said.

8

Darek followed his old friend Mizzle down the dark mountainside. Zantor had been left behind, much to his dismay. His scent would have warned the Red Fangs of their approach. Following close behind Darek came Zarnak, Horek, and a couple dozen of their best warriors. Mizzle watched over his shoulder. Each time Zarnak dropped back out of earshot, he spoke.

"Mizzle no like Zarnak," he said quietly.

Darek smiled. "Me neither," he said. "But he's got all the power right now."

"What be power?" asked Mizzle.

"It's how people make others do things," said Darek.

"Power bad," said Mizzle.

"Not always," said Darek. "But it's bad if a cruel person has it."

"Like Zahr?" said Mizzle.

"Yes. Like Zahr, and Rebbe, and Zarnak. I'm beginning to think they're all cut from the same mold."

"But Zarnak not be Kraden," said Mizzle.

Darek nodded. "I know. But it seems that perhaps Kradens and Zorians aren't so . . ."

"So what?" asked Mizzle.

"So different," Darek added thoughtfully. "So different after all."

"How close are we?" came a loud whisper.

"Be close," Mizzle called to Zarnak. "Be very close."

They began to hear the rustlings of the sleeping dragons. An occasional belch of flame brightened the night. At last the great cage loomed before them. Darek's heart thumped. The Reds were beautiful, their scales glowing pure white in the moonlight. They looked peaceful in sleep. Only their bloodred fangs gave away their fierce nature.

Mizzle coughed. "Guards be there, there, and there." He pointed, then coughed again.

"Thanks, little friend," said Darek. "You'd better get back now. The mist isn't thick enough for you here."

"Good luck, Dragon Boy," said Mizzle. "Be ye careful."

"I will," said Darek. But inside he was frightened. He knew he'd be lucky to get through this night alive.

Mizzle scurried away into the darkness, just as Zarnak and Horek came up.

"Where are they?" Zarnak asked.

Darek pointed out the guard positions. Zarnak nodded, then sent Horek and the men forward. Zarnak and Darek watched as the men slipped through the shadows toward the unsuspecting guards.

"They'll never know what hit them," Zarnak said with a chuckle.

Darek swallowed hard. He should be glad. The Kradens had been cruel to him and to the other slaves. But his own words kept echoing in his ears.

Perhaps Kradens and Zorians aren't so different after all. Maybe there were good Kradens and bad Kradens, just like there were good and bad Zorians. What if some of these men were the good ones? What if they were fathers, with children waiting at home? What if . . .

Darek heard a gasp and a strangled cry. Then another. One by one the dark shapes of the Kradens slumped to the ground. Darek swallowed again and looked away.

Horek scrambled back up the hill. "The guards are taken care of, sire," he said. "But we'd better move fast. No telling when the watch changes." Zarnak nodded. The plan was to get the dragons out of the cage and up into the mountains where the Kradens couldn't follow. Darek, who had a way with dragons, was to go in first and try to get a harness on the lead male. If he was successful, the other dragons would follow. If he failed . . . Darek sucked in a deep breath. No sense dwelling on what would happen if he failed.

"Ready, *Dragon Boy?*" Zarnak asked sarcastically.

Darek didn't smile. He followed Horek down the hill to the cage. The Reds were waking up, aroused by the scuffle with the guards, no doubt. They paced fretfully in their cage, sniffing the air, bellowing their anger at being disturbed. Soon their roars would be heard in town. Then Zahr's men would ride out to investigate. Time was growing short.

Horek handed Darek a harness. "When we pull the doors open," he said, "you go in. The lead male will be the first to approach."

Darek nodded, then slung the harness over his shoulder.

"Open the doors," he said.

9

Darek willed his heart to stop pounding. The dragons would sense his fear. He had to remain calm. The herd had backed off upon his entrance. They milled fretfully, tossing their heads, snorting an occasional blast of flame. Darek watched, trying to pick out the lead male, trying to be ready when the beast made its move. Just then one of the largest males locked eyes with him. Darek stared back, trying not to flinch. He attempted to send a mind message, the way he did with Zantor, a calm, soothing mind message.

The male moved toward him, slowly. *Easy,* Darek said with his mind. *Easy. I won't hurt you.* The beast came on, head down, eyes fixed on Darek's. Slowly Darek slid the harness off his shoulder and held it out.

"Easy," he said softly. "We're just going to take a little ride."

Then, without warning, the dragon reared! When it crashed down again, flames shot from its mouth. Its eyes blazed. Darek froze.

GRRAWWWK! screamed the beast. Then it charged!

It all happened so fast, Darek couldn't think. First the blast of flame. Then he was hurled into the air. His head hit the roof of the cage. But before he fell to the ground he was caught and whipped around once more. His neck snapped painfully. He saw claws slashing, fangs flashing. He flailed with his arms, kicked with his legs. But it was no use. His body was launched into the air again. This time he hit the side of the cage and crashed to the ground in a crumpled heap.

GRRAWWWK! Another earsplitting scream. Darek looked up but couldn't see. Blood ran in his eyes. With a trembling hand he wiped it away, waiting to see the Red bearing down again. Instead, he saw a blur of white and red . . . and blue!

"Zantor!" he cried.

If Zantor heard him, he gave no sign. He couldn't. He was locked in a battle for his life. Darek watched with pounding heart as the dragons reared and charged, then reared and charged again. The other dragons watched, too, in hushed silence. This was a duel of kings. Bursts of fire flashed in the night. Screams of fury echoed off the mountains. The two clashed again, and when they came apart, both were bloodied.

Darek winced. Strange and terrible thoughts raced through his mind. Zantor's thoughts. Thoughts he'd never known the gentle creature capable of. The battle raged on. Both beasts were wounded. Both were tiring. Darek closed his eyes and prayed, prayed for the life of his beloved

friend. At last there came a piteous scream and Darek bit his lip. Slowly, he opened his eyes.

There on the ground lay the Red. His neck was pinned to the earth by Zantor's great jaws. His body was slack, but his great sides still heaved.

Darek received a terrible mind message. *Kill*, it said clearly. *Kill!* Darek closed his eyes and sent a message back.

No, Zantor, he said. *Don't kill. You have won. He is beaten. There is no need to kill.*

Slowly Zantor released his death grip. The Red struggled to its feet and dragged itself away. The other dragons closed in around Zantor and began licking his wounds. Clearly they had accepted him as their new leader.

Darek limped out and threw his arms around Zantor's bowed neck. "You *are* King of the Dragons, Zantor," he whispered. "But to me you're even more. You're the best friend anyone could ever have.

"*Thrummm*," sang Zantor wearily. "*Thrummm, thrummm, thrummm.*"

10

The Red Fangs had followed Zantor willingly into the mountains and Zarnak was well pleased. So pleased that Darek dared to approach him the next morning as he stood watching the training exercises.

"Sire?" said Darek.

Zarnak looked down.

"Ah, young Darek," he said with surprising warmth. "How are your bruises this morning?"

"Better, sire, thank you."

"And the dragon? How is he?"

"Well, sire. Those Reds must have powerful

medicine in their tongues. His wounds are nearly
healed."

"Good. Good. He's quite a beast."

"Yes, sire." Darek smiled, then he shook his

head in wonderment. "I still can't believe the Reds accepted him that way."

"Oh, that's not so strange," said Zarnak. "The two breeds are very close. They've even been known to interbreed. Haven't you ever heard of Purple Spiked dragons?"

"Yes," said Darek. "Grandfather used to speak of them. But I never knew they were of mixed blood."

"They are. Part Red, part Blue."

Darek pondered this a moment. "It makes sense," he said at last. "My grandfather said they were very rare and very fierce."

"Yes." Zarnak sighed heavily. "Very fierce. My father and grandfather were killed by one, just days before I was born. I never knew either of them."

"I'm sorry," said Darek.

Zarnak nodded. "So am I. My grandfather was Chief Elder at the time. That's when the throne passed out of our family."

"Is that why you're so bent on getting it back?" asked Darek.

Zarnak stared straight ahead. "Yes," he said. "It belongs to me."

"But," Darek began, "you weren't born—"

"Enough!" snapped Zarnak. "You're spoiling my good humor. The past is past. I like the present better." He rubbed his hands together. "I gather from the noise and activity down in Krad that Zahr has discovered his empty dragon cage."

"Yes, sire," said Darek. "That's what I came to talk about."

"Oh?" Zarnak looked down at him again.

"Yes, sire. I was thinking that, without dragons, Zahr is in a very bad position."

"Yes." Zarnak chuckled. "Very bad indeed."

"So bad," Darek went on, "that he might be willing to talk."

"Talk?" said Zarnak. "Why would we want to talk? We've got the upper hand."

"But there will be bloodshed," said Darek. "Zahr is weakened without his dragons, but he

56

won't go down without a fight. And he'll take all the Zorians he can with him."

Zarnak did not seem concerned. "War is war," he said with a flick of his hand. "Men die."

Darek felt anger stir within him. *But not you, Zarnak,* he thought bitterly. *You will sit safe on your mountaintop and send others to their deaths.* He bit his tongue and turned to watch the training exercises. He knew many of these men. They were good men. Some of them were little more than boys. Back home their wives and mothers waited, praying prayers and shedding tears. How could Zarnak not care? Had his own loss hardened his heart? Did he think it only fair for others to suffer as he and his mother had? There must be some way to get to him. If not through his heart . . . then perhaps through his greed.

"You're right, Zarnak," said Darek. "Men do die in wars. But think what a hero you would be if all of these men came home safely. Imagine if you, Zarnak, could rescue the slaves without spilling a drop of Zorian blood. They would restore you to the throne for certain. They'd build monuments to you. Balladeers would sing your name. Why, Zoriak might even be renamed Zarnak."

Zarnak was listening now. He cocked his head and gave Darek a searching look.

"What do you have in mind?" he asked.

"Let me take Zantor and fly to Zahr's castle. Let me bargain with him. If he releases the slaves, we leave in peace."

"And what if Zahr decides to pursue us?"

"He can't. He can't get through the mist."

"He can if he figures out how to make battle masks."

"That could take years," said Darek.

"Or months. Or weeks." Zarnak shook his head. "No," he said firmly. "It's too risky. If we don't finish him now, we'll be forever looking over our shoulders."

11

Darek sat on a log between Pola and Rowena. The campfire flickered on their faces. Mizzle sat in the dirt by their feet, playing with a small, round stone. Zarnak came back from meeting with some of his men. He was in a jovial mood.

"Break out a barrel of slog," he called to one of the guards. "We shall celebrate tonight, for tomorrow Krad will be ours."

Tomorrow. Darek sighed heavily. He had hoped for more time to work on Zarnak, to get him to reconsider.

Azzon sat nearby, chained to a large rock. At Zarnak's words he had looked up briefly, then returned to staring sadly into the fire. *Poor Azzon,* thought Darek. *Up here away from his cave and his potions . . .*

Suddenly Darek's heart beat faster. Azzon's potions! Why hadn't he thought of them?

"Mizzle," he whispered under his breath.

Mizzle looked up at him.

"Don't look at me," said Darek. "Just listen."

Mizzle went back to playing with his stone, but he cocked an ear in Darek's direction.

"Go to Azzon's cave," said Darek. "Get the memory potion. Bring it back here. When no one is looking, dump it in the barrel of slog."

Mizzle sat quietly rolling his rock back and forth for another moment. Then he gave it an extra push and it started to roll down the mountainside. He scampered after it. Darek glanced at Pola and Rowena and smiled.

"What are you up to?" whispered Rowena.

"You'll see," said Darek.

Before long, Mizzle was back with the vial hidden under his arm. Dear Mizzle. He must have run like the wind. The barrel of slog had just been rolled up. Mizzle hopped around it, curiously. As soon as the lid was pried off, he jumped to the rim.

61

"Me try," he said, leaning over the foaming brew and pretending to drink.

"Zatz!" shouted Zarnak. "Get out of there!" Mizzle jumped down and scampered away, twittering merrily. "Glog good!" he cried. "Glog good." As he scampered past Darek, he winked one of his great, yellow-green eyes.

Zarnak called the guards up to dip their mugs. Then Zarnak dipped a mug for himself and sat down. Horek did the same. Zarnak lifted his mug to Horek's.

"To victory!" he said.

"To victory!" Horek returned. They clinked mugs and downed the glog.

"Ah," said Zarnak, wiping the foam from his mouth. "An excellent batch."

"Mmmm," Horek agreed, smacking his lips.

Darek watched closely. Before long Zarnak and Horek began to shrink! Their faces were growing younger and younger. Next moment Horek grabbed the crown off Zarnak's head.

"You always get to be Chief Elder," he cried in a whiny voice. "It's my turn now!"

"*No!*" Zarnak grabbed the crown back and they both started tugging.

Horek kicked dirt at Zarnak.

"Quit it, you meanie!" cried Zarnak. He pulled the crown free and whacked Horek over the head with it. All the while they were continuing to shrink. Soon two wailing toddlers sat tugging at their battle masks and struggling under a pile of oversized clothes.

Darek stared openmouthed. Azzon threw his head back and laughed.

"What the . . . ?" said Pola.

"How did you do that?" Rowena asked Darek.

Darek looked around at the guards, who had turned into toddlers, too. Then he started to laugh.

"I sent Mizzle for Azzon's memory potion," he said. "I told him to dump it in the slog. Looks like he brought the youth potion instead."

"Oop!" said Mizzle.

"No matter," said Darek. "This'll do the job. They won't be back to their normal selves for a couple of days."

"Probably even longer," said Azzon. "The alcohol in the slog will strengthen the potion."

"All the better," said Darek. "That'll give me plenty of time."

"To do what?" asked Rowena.

"To go see Zahr," said Darek. "To see if I can get him to surrender the slaves without bloodshed."

Azzon shook his head. "You're wasting your time," he said. "My son would rather die than surrender."

"Well, I've got to try," said Darek. "What is there to lose?"

"Your life," said Azzon. "Don't be a fool."

"A lot more lives will be lost if I don't try," said Darek. "Now, I've got to go. With the racket these babies are making, the other men will soon be up to investigate." He took a key from Zarnak's ring and unlocked Azzon's chains. Azzon pulled a ring from his finger and held it out to Darek. "Take this," he said. "Give it to Zahr. Tell him . . . tell him that I love him, and Rebbe, too. Tell him I'd like another chance to be their father."

"Why don't you come along and tell him yourself?" asked Darek.

Azzon shook his head. "Zahr would likely kill me before I got the words out. But if he will listen to you . . . if he will give me a chance . . . then I will come. Tell him to hoist a red flag from the main turret of the castle and I will come, alone and unarmed."

"What if he tricks you?" asked Darek. "What if he flies the flag and then kills you?"

Azzon looked down. "If he wants me dead," he said, "even knowing how I love him, then so be it."

Darek nodded slowly. "I will deliver your message," he said. He slipped the ring onto his thumb, then turned to Pola and Rowena.

"Give me two days," he said, "no matter *what*

happens, unless you know with certainty that I am dead. Do not come for me until then."

Pola and Rowena nodded. "What of the other men?" asked Pola.

"Stall them," said Darek. "Tell them I'm talking with Zahr, trying to free the slaves peacefully. Without Zarnak to egg them on, I think they'll wait."

Pola and Rowena each reached out an arm. Darek clasped them both in a brotherhood shake.

"Lord Eternal go with you," said Pola and Rowena.

"And with you," Darek returned.

"Boo-boo," wailed Zarnak. He held up a bloodied little finger.

Darek winked at Pola and Rowena. "Keep an eye on the *kids*," he said. "I'll be back as soon as I can."

12

Zantor was flying strongly. The night air was warm and damp. They were out of the mists now and the lights of Krad flickered ahead. Darek had left his battle mask behind. He wouldn't need it in Krad. Besides, if things went badly, he didn't want it to fall into the wrong hands. Now that he was on his way, he was scared. Really scared. It was one thing to talk of bravery, another actually to be brave. More than anything he wanted to turn back the clock, just to be a child again, at home with his mother, father, and Clep. But the clock didn't go backward. And even if it did, how could he go back and turn a blind eye to truth, let the dragon quests go on, let men and dragons die for nothing? *An adventure's an adventure, all the way to the end.* Yes. This adventure had a life of its own now. Wherever it led, he must follow.

As the city loomed closer, Darek's heart beat faster. There was unusual activity in the streets. People milled about and torches blazed. The turrets of Castle Krad were torchlit, too. Before long an alarm sounded. Darek and Zantor had been spotted.

The streets quickly emptied and warriors poured onto the battlements of Castle Krad. The moonlight glinted off their armor as they hastened to fit arrows to their bows. But before the first arrow could loft into the air, Darek gave the command.

"Down, Zantor."

Zantor tilted his wings and circled down into the center of the castle courtyard. Warriors

poured into the courtyard from all sides. A forest of arrows pointed at Zantor. Darek looked up and saw a second tier of arrows aiming down from the battlements.

"Easy, Zantor," Darek murmured. "Stay calm. Stay still."

Darek stared around him at the sea of hostile faces.

"I come in peace," he shouted. "I come to bargain with Zahr."

Straight ahead, a great flight of steps went up to a set of huge double doors. These swung slowly open now, and a tall Kraden appeared. He wore a crown and a long red robe that billowed out behind him. He walked to the edge of the steps, then stopped and stared at Darek. Darek shivered. So this was the mighty Zahr. The resemblance to Azzon was striking, except that this man's features were hardened by hate. Suddenly Zahr threw his head back and laughed.

"A *boy!*" he shouted. "The Zorians send a *boy* to bargain with the mighty Zahr?"

71

Darek bristled. "I'm not *just* a boy," he said loudly. "I'm the boy who escaped from your dragon nurseries. I'm the boy who rescued the Zorian prisoners from your mines. *I'm the boy who stole your dragons.* I am Darek of Zoriac."

Zahr's smile faded. "Come forward," he said.

Darek stroked Zantor's neck. "Stay," he said.

Grrawwwk, came a sharp mind cry.

"I'll be okay," said Darek. "Just wait here." Then he slid down Zantor's back to the ground. The warriors parted and Darek walked between them and mounted the steps. As soon as he reached the top, Zahr nodded to his guards.

"Seize him," he said. Two men lunged and grabbed Darek. Instantly Zantor reared, but just as instantly Zahr responded.

"KILL THE DRAGON!" he bellowed.

"NO!" Darek screamed. He turned to Zantor and shouted, "FLY, ZANTOR! Fly back to the mountains!"

Zantor sprang into the air, but a volley of arrows followed him. Darek winced as he saw several hit their mark. Images of terror and pain flooded Darek's head. Zantor's wings missed a beat, and for a moment it looked like he would fall. But then he rose again and cleared the castle walls.

"After him!" boomed Zahr.

Hordes of soldiers streamed out of the courtyard in pursuit of the dragon. Darek closed his eyes and sent the strongest mind message he could. *Fly! Fly! Fly for all you're worth!*

Messages of fear and pain still crowded into Darek's head long after Zantor disappeared. But that was all right. As long as the messages kept coming, Zantor was alive.

And then, suddenly, they stopped.

13

Darek stood chained against a cold cell wall. His arms were drawn up over his head so tightly that his toes barely touched the floor. He'd been dangling like that for hours. Maybe days. He didn't know. He didn't care. He only cared about one thing. Zantor. Why wasn't he sending messages? Why wasn't he answering Darek's silent pleas?

The cell door banged open and someone strode in. Darek looked up. It was Zahr, and he had a whip in his hand.

"Well, well," he said. "Ready to talk?"

"What happened to my dragon?" asked Darek.

"I had him made into a wall hanging," said Zahr. His cold eyes glittered like ice.

"You're lying!" Darek spat. "He's still alive. I know he is!"

"Do you now?" Zahr pulled at his chin. "And just *how* do you know it?"

Darek swallowed hard. *Zantor,* he cried inside his head. *Zantor, answer me.* But no answer came.

Zahr threw his head back and laughed. "I'll tell you what happened to your dragon," he said. "But first you tell me why your friends stole mine."

Darek bit his lip.

"Tell me what they want!" Zahr bellowed.

"They want the slaves," Darek said. "All of them. And they don't care who they have to kill to get them."

Zahr chuckled. "I thought as much," he said. "Well, let them come."

Darek stared at him. "They've got the dragons," he said. "You don't stand a chance."

Zahr chuckled again. "You underestimate me," he said. "A rider has been sent to my brother. He will arrive with his armies and dragons at any moment."

"I thought your brother was your enemy," said Darek.

Zahr laughed. "Maybe so," he said, "but he knows if I fall, he'll be next." Then Zahr's eyes narrowed. "How do you know about my brother?" he asked.

"Your father told me," said Darek.

The color drained from Zahr's face.

"My father . . . is dead," he said.

"No," said Darek. "Your father lives—in a cave under the Black Mountains."

Zahr took a step back.

"That's a lie," he said. "He can't be alive."

"He can be, and he is," said Darek. "He asked me to give you his ring." Darek pulled the great ring from his thumb and held it out to Zahr.

Zahr gasped, then clutched the ring and turned away. But not before Darek saw the wetness in his eyes.

"How do I know you're telling the truth?" Zahr cried. "How do I know the Zynots didn't find this ring on my father's body and give it to you?"

"Your father told me many things," said Darek, "about you and Rebbe. How he used to pit you against one another when you were boys and make you fight. How he used to beat the loser and send him to bed without supper."

Zahr whirled. His eyes blazed.

"Yes," he said. "And the loser was always me. The smaller one. But not anymore. I'm Zahr now. King of Krad. Envy of all men!"

Darek shook his head. "I don't envy you," he said. "Your brother is your enemy. Your father lives in fear of you. What joy does your kingdom bring?"

Zahr sneered. "Joy?" he said. "What is joy? How can one miss what one has never known?"

"You can know it now, Zahr," said Darek quietly. "Your father asked me to tell you he's sorry."

Zahr snorted. "Sorry!" he said. "He's sorry I beat him, that's all. Sorry that I'm king now, and he is nothing."

"No," said Darek. "He's content to be nothing. He doesn't want to be king. But there is one thing that he wants."

"Ahh," said Zahr, "and what would that be?"

"A chance to be a real father to you and Rebbe."

Zahr stared at Darek for long moment, then slowly shook his head. "It's too late for that," he said. "I don't need him anymore."

"I don't believe you," said Darek.

"What do you know of me?" asked Zahr.

"I know . . . I think . . . that on the inside you're not so different from me," said Darek. "And I know I need my father. And I miss him."

Zahr turned away and stared out the window. After a long silence he asked, "What else did he say?"

"He said . . . he loves you."

Zahr whirled once more. "Now I know you're lying," he said. "My father *never* spoke those words to me. Never in my life."

"He is waiting to speak them now," said Darek. "All you need do is hoist a red flag from the highest turret. Then he will come, alone and unarmed. And he will tell you for himself."

14

Azzon looked regal in his royal robes. Zahr and Rebbe stood on either side of him. Their sharp features were gentled by smiles. Gazing out over the cheering throng of newly freed slaves, they looked almost kind. Darek shook his head in wonder. It was a powerful force—a father's love.

It was a glorious day. A day to rejoice. A messenger had been sent back to Zoriac to free Darek's and Rowena's fathers and bring them to Krad to work out the details of the peace settlement. It would take time, Darek knew, but he couldn't

help feeling that this was the start of a bright new future for all—dragons, Zorians, Kradens, and, yes, even the little Zynots. Only one thing still worried Darek. Zantor. Darek still hadn't learned the dragon's fate. Zahr had told him that Zantor had been wounded, but that he had made it back to the Black Mountains. But then why were there still no mind messages? Darek had tried to find a moment to question Azzon, but Azzon had been busy with his sons since his arrival.

"Look! In the sky!" someone shouted.

Darek looked up. Two Great Blue dragons were winging their way down into the courtyard. Drizba and Typra! And they were bearing Pola and Rowena. The crowd parted to let them land. In spite of his worries, Darek smiled. Rowena slid out of her saddle and rushed into his arms.

"Oh, Darek!" she cried. "It's so wonderful!"

"Yes," said Darek, one eye still on the sky. "But where is . . ."

Suddenly Pola rushed up and clapped Darek on

the back. "You did it, my friend," he said. "You really did it!"

Darek smiled. "We all did it," he said. "But where is . . ."

Just then Darek heard a sound, a faint sort of hum. A faint sort of *thrummm!* He whirled and looked. There, peeking out of Drizba's pouch, was the tiny blue head of a newborn dragonling! Darek's mouth dropped open. But . . . that was impossible. Drizba was too young to mate.

"What is that?" Darek asked, pointing. The little creature had climbed out of the pouch and was approaching on wobbly legs.

"Didn't Azzon tell you?" asked Rowena.

"Tell me what?" asked Darek. His eyes were riveted on the baby dragon. Warm, joyful feelings were filling his mind. All at once he knew!

"Zantor!" he cried. He ran to the dragonling and swept it up. The tiny tongue flicked out and kissed his cheek. Tears of joy welled in Darek's eyes. He hugged the dragonling tight, too overwhelmed to speak. At last he turned to Rowena and asked, "How?"

Rowena smiled. "He was badly wounded when he got back to the mountains," she said. "Azzon said he wasn't going to live because his body was so large and his heart so weak."

"So Azzon gave him the youth potion," Pola put in. "It shrank him down to a size his heart could manage. It shrank his wounds, too. Now they're only pinpricks."

"So, he's going to be okay?" said Darek.

Rowena smiled. "Yes," she said, stroking the nubby little head. "He's been doing a lot of sleeping. But he's going to be just fine."

"There's only one problem," said Pola. "Azzon had to give him such a strong dose that the aging process was completely reversed."

"What does that mean?" asked Darek.

"It means he's going to have to grow up all over again," said Rowena. "Do you think you're ready to raise a baby dragon again?"

Darek thought back over all Zantor's exploits of the past year, then he laughed. "Hey," he said, looking into the dragon's wide green eyes, "an adventure's an adventure, all the way to the end. Isn't it, little Dragon King?"

Zantor snuggled happily in Darek's arms. "*Thrummm*," he sang. "*Thrummm, thrummm, thrummm.*"

About the Author

Jackie French Koller is the award-winning author of nearly twenty books for children and young adults. She started the *Dragonling* series at the request of her youngest son, Devin, then in the third grade, because dragons were his "second favorite animals—next to dogs."

About the Illustrator

Judith Mitchell has been an illustrator for some time, and has drawn and painted mermaids, trolls, griffins, fairies, Martians, monsters and—dragons! Dragons are special; Zantor is her favorite. Judith lives in New York City, where there is the subway, and near the ocean in Maine, where she suspects there are sea serpents. Recently she married the handsomest man in the world.